SQUARE
FISH

An Imprint of Macmillan

AND IF THE MOON COULD TALK. Text copyright © 1998 by Kate Banks.
Pictures copyright © 1997 by Georg Hallensleben. All rights reserved.
Printed in China by South China Printing Company Ltd., Dongguan City, Guangdong Province.
For information, address Square Fish, 175 Fifth Avenue, New York, NY 10010.

Square Fish and the Square Fish logo are trademarks of Macmillan and
are used by Farrar Straus Giroux under license from Macmillan.

Library of Congress Cataloging-in-Publication Data
Banks, Kate, 1960–
And if the moon could talk / Kate Banks ; pictures by Georg Hallensleben.
p.   cm.
Summary: As evening progresses into nighttime, the moon looks down on a variety of nocturnal scenes,
including a child getting ready for bed.
ISBN 978-0-374-43558-5
[1. Bedtime—Fiction. 2. Night—Fiction. 3. Moon—Fiction.] I. Hallensleben, Georg, ill. II. Title.
PZ7.B22594An 1998   [E]—dc21   97-29770

Originally published in France by Gallimard Jeunesse, 1997
First published in the United States by Farrar Straus Giroux, 1998
First Square Fish Edition: January 2013
Square Fish logo designed by Filomena Tuosto
mackids.com

10 9 8 7 6 5 4

AR: 2.6

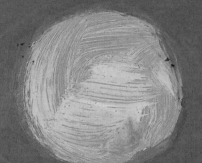

And If the Moon Could Talk

Kate Banks • Pictures by Georg Hallensleben

SQUARE
FISH

FARRAR STRAUS GIROUX

NEW YORK

Somewhere a pair of shoes lies under a chair.

A window yawns open. Twilight blazes a trail across the wall.

And if the moon could talk,
it would tell of evening
stealing through the woods
and a lizard scurrying home to supper.

Someone hums quietly. A clock ticks. A light flicks on.

And if the moon could talk,
it would tell of stars flaring up one by one
and a small fire burning by a tree.

Papa opens a book and turns the pages.

A story unfolds like a banner wandering across the sky.

And if the moon could talk,
it would tell of sand blowing across the desert
and nomads crouching by the dune.

On a small table sits a glass, a wooden boat, a starfish, too.

And if the moon could talk,
it would tell of waves washing onto the beach,
shells, and a crab resting.

Music chimes from a small box on a shelf. A mobile stirs the air.

On a chair, a rabbit sits listening.

And if the moon could talk,
it would tell of the wind rocking a tree
and a bird safe in its nest.

Mama hands her child the rabbit.

She hugs her and pulls the blankets tight under her chin.

And if the moon could talk,
it would tell of a faraway den
and a lion licking her cubs.

Eyes close. There is a drowsy hush.

Darkness swells into a colorful dream.

And if the moon could talk,
it would tell of a child
curled up in bed wrapped in sleep.

And it would murmur

Good night.